King's Head Th

BIZET'S
CARMEN

in a new English version by
Mary Franklin & Ashley Pearson

This production officially opened at the King's Head Theatre on Wednesday 13 February 2019

Georges Bizet's *Carmen* in a new version by Ashley Pearson and Mary Franklin was first performed at the King's Head Theatre, London on 6 February 2019 with the following cast:

Cast
CARMEN – Ellie Edmonds
CARMEN – Jane Monari
JOSE – Mike Bradley
JOSE – Roger Paterson
ESCAMILLIO – Dan D'Souza

Production Team
Director & Co-librettist – Mary Franklin
Co-librettist – Ashley Pearson
Musical Director – Juliane Gallant
Designer – Anna Lewis
Lighting Designer – David Doyle
Sound Designer – David Eaton
Movement Director – Jennifer Fletcher
Assistant Director – Alexandria Anfield

Producer – Louisa Davis

Production Manager – Colin Everitt
Stage Manager – Octavia Peneş
Assistant Producer – Alexander Hick

CAST

Ellie Edmonds – Carmen

British Mezzo Soprano Ellie Edmonds trained at Chethams School of Music and Birmingham Conservatoire with Christine Cairns, where she won numerous prizes and awards. She went on to complete her Masters degree at WIAV where she was a student of Dennis O'Niell.

Recent Operatic roles include Zaida in *Il turco in Italia* (Proper Opera); Ottavia in *L'incorinazione di Poppea* (Berlin Opera Academy); Annina in *La Traviata* (Opera Holland Park) and Natalia in Leoncavallo's *Zazà* (Opera Holland Park).

Ellie made her Royal Opera House debut in the role of Victorian in Opera Holland Park's *Alice's Adventures in Wonderland* by Will Todd, which was performed at the Linbury Studio in November 2015. She is looking forward to a return to Opera Holland Park as Un Musico in *Manon Lescaut* in summer 2019.

Ellie enjoys an active outreach work schedule, recently including Chorus Mentoring at Birmingham Opera Company for WAKE (Battistelli); workshopping Opera with Royal Opera House/ Graeae Theatre Company, and continuing work with Opera Holland Park's internationally award winning *Inspire* program.
www.ellieedmonds.com

Jane Monari – Carmen

American Mezzo Soprano Jane Monari hails from Philadelphia. Jane previously completed a Bachelor's of Music in Voice Performance, with Scholastic Distinction, at the Juilliard School. Jane also completed the Master of Arts degree, with Distinction and a DipRAM, at the Royal Academy of Music. She is a graduate of the Alexander Gibson Opera School at the Royal Conservatoire of Scotland. Jane has appeared as a soloist in concert, singing Händel's *Israel in Egypt*, the Beethoven *Missa Solemnis*, the Mozart *Requiem*, and *Die Erste Walpurgisnacht* by Mendelssohn (City of Glasgow Chorus and the Orchestra of Scottish Opera).

Jane's operatic roles include The Page in *Rigoletto* (Scottish Opera); The Prince in *Cendrillon* (Fife Opera); Popova in *The Bear* (Royal Conservatoire of Scotland); The Sorceress in *Dido and Aeneas*

(Royal Conservatoire of Scotland); The Witch in *Hänsel and Gretel* (Opera Holloway); La Ciesca in *Gianni Schicchi* (Juilliard School); Hermia in *A Midsummer Night's Dream* (Juilliard School); Veronica in *Sunday Excursion* (Juilliard School); Sally in *A Hand of Bridge* (Juilliard School); and The Maid in *Schwergewicht* (Juilliard School).

Mike Bradley – Jose

Mike Bradley trained as a Tenor, at the Guildhall School of Music and Drama, under Adrian Thompson.

Credits include Lensky in *Eugene Onegin* (Opera Up Close); Triquet in *Eugene Onegin* (Opera Up Close); Augusto in *Zazà* (Opera Holland Park); Boatman in *Kát'a Kabanová* (Opera Holland Park); Victorian Tenor in *Alice's Adventures in Wonderland* (Opera Holland Park); Parpignol in *La bohème* (Opera Holland Park); Merciaiuolo in *Iris* (Opera Holland Park); Chinois in *Lakmé* (Opera Holland Park); Rodolfo in *La bohème* (Merry Opera Company); Postiglione in *La fanciulla del West* (Opera Holland Park); Venditore di Canzonette and Tenore Amante in *Il tabarro* (Fulham Opera); and has recently performed in a 12 voice staged production of Verdi's *Requiem* (Merry Opera Company).

Mike will be returning to Opera Holland Park this Summer to sing in the chorus of *Manon Lescaut* and *Un ballo in maschera*, in which he will also be performing the role of Un servo del Conte. In 2020, Mike once again returns to Opera Holland Park and will be performing the role of Borsa in Verdi's *Rigoletto*.

Roger Paterson – Jose

Roger Paterson's music training began at the Junior Academy of Music at the Royal Conservatoire of Scotland (RCS) and continued at the University of Glasgow where he gained an honours degree in Musicology in 2007. Since then, he commenced his singing studies with Joan Gordon, Pat McMahon and Paul Farrington. In 2009, he was employed as the music director for 'The Come Back to God' missionary society and also began teaching music privately with all ages from 4 years onwards teenagers, college and university students, adults of different ages and professions. He did this for six years and meanwhile, in 2013, started giving recitals as a classical singer. From 2014, he became a founding member of Scozzesi, with whom he has been performing across Scotland.

Since 2015, Roger has been a full-time opera singer performing the roles: Mozart in the Off WestEnd Awarded nominated *Mozart and Salieri*, Cavaradossi in the Off WestEnd Award-winning *Tosca*, Rodolfo in the Olivier nominated *La bohème*, the role of Giuseppe and cover of the role of Gaston in *La Traviata* (Longborough Festival Opera). This year, 2019, Roger will play Don Jose in the King's Head Theatre's brand new production of *Carmen*, he will return to the role of Count Almaviva in Opera Brava's production of *Il barbiere di Siviglia*, and also play the role of Alfredo in their brand new production of *La Traviata*. His plans also include opera galas, concerts with Scozzesi, Opera Alba and Coro Alba.

Dan D'Souza – Escamillio

'Burnished baritone' Dan D'Souza (*The Stage*) was educated at the Royal College of Music and the University of Cambridge. In 2019, he resumes studies on the world-renowned Guildhall School of Music and Drama Opera Course.

Recent roles include Conte Perrucchetto in *La Fedeltà Premiata* (Royal Opera House Mumbai); Count Robinson in *Secret Marriage* (Hampstead Garden Opera); Starveling in *A Midsummer Night's Dream* (Royal College of Music International Opera School) and Pig in *The Enchanted Pig* (Hampstead Garden Opera). In 2019, he will make his debut at La Scala singing Priest in *Semele* under the baton of Sir John Eliot Gardiner.

As a recitalist, Dan performs across the UK with varied and creative programmes of lesser known and new songs. He is the 2018 winner of both the Dame Patricia Routledge National English Song Competition and the Royal College of Music Lieder Competition. He is an Associate Artist for Salon Opera, an Iford Arts New Generation Artist, and a Southrepps Festival Young Artist.

www.dandsouza.com

PRODUCTION TEAM

Mary Franklin – Director & Co-librettist

Mary is the Artistic Director and Co-Founder of Rough Haired Pointer. Education includes BA Hons in English Literature (Oxford University).

Directing credits include *The Diary Of A Nobody* (King's Head Theatre, White Bear Theatre); the World Premiere of Joe Orton's *Fred & Madge* (Hope Theatre); *I Do Need Me* (Tête à Tête); *Boy* (Arcola Theatre); *Christie In Love* (King's Head Theatre); *The Young Visiters* (Tabard Theatre, Hen and Chickens Theatre); *Noonday Demons* (King's Head Theatre); *Murder On The Trading Floor* (Tabard Theatre); Madame Manet (Tabard Theatre); *Marco Polo* (Hen and Chickens Theatre); *The Boy Who Cried* (Hope Theatre, Tabard Theatre) and *Cleopatra* (King's Head Theatre, Hope Theatre).

Assistant directing includes *La Traviata* (Opera Holland Park); *Blown Away* (Lyric Hammersmith); *Tosca* (Soho Theatre, UK Tour); *Quasimodo* (King's Head Theatre); *Filter* (Sadler's Wells); *Arab Nights* (Soho Theatre) and *The Invention Of Love* (Oxford Playhouse).

Ashley Pearson – Co-librettist

Ashley Pearson is a Canadian writer and director based in London. Her directing work includes *Don Giovanni* (Opera On Location); *Così fan tutte, Orpheus in the Underworld, Die Zauberflöte* (St. Paul's Opera); *Nerves of the Heart* (Quest); *Woyzeck* (Powerhouse Theatre).

Her work as a writer and librettist includes *Music Oft Hath Such a Charm* (OperaUpClose, UK Tour); *League of Youth, Coverage* (Riot Act); *Mary, Mary* (Theatre Mensch).

Ashley was Associate Director of the 2017 Opera Works programme at the English National Opera. Her work as an Assistant Director includes *Macbeth* (Royal Opera House); *Les Mamelles de Tirésias, Une Éducation Manquée* (Royal College of Music); *Don Giovanni, Die Fledermaus* (Lyric Opera Studio Weimar); *Carmen, La Traviata, Ulla's Odyssey* (OperaUpClose, UK tour).

Ashley holds an MFA in Theatre Directing from East 15 Acting School. She was an apprentice director with New York Stage and Film's Powerhouse Theatre Festival and holds a BASc specializing in theatre, abstract mathematics, and film studies from Quest University Canada. She was also a literary researcher for the Ustinov Studio at the Theatre Royal, Bath.

Juliane Gallant – Musical Director

Juliane Gallant is accomplished in both operatic and song repertoire, working as musical director, repetiteur, accompanist, coach and conductor. She studied Piano Accompaniment with Pamela Lidiard at the Guildhall School of Music and Drama. She also holds degrees from the Université de Moncton, the University of Ottawa, and the Conservatoire de musique et d'art dramatique de Montréal. In September 2018, Juliane was one of only twelve conductors selected for the Women Conductors Course: Conducting for Opera, run by the Royal Opera House, the National Opera Studio and the Royal Philharmonic Society.

Juliane has worked as musical director for *A Fantastic Bohemian: The Tales of Hoffmann revisited* (Opera Mio); *Carmen* (Opera on Location, Opera Up Close); *Così fan tutte* (St Paul's Opera); *Don Giovanni* (Opera on Location); *La bohème* (Clapham Opera Festival); *Orphée aux enfers* (St Paul's Opera). She has also served as repetiteur for *The Medium* (Magnetic Opera); *Il barbiere di Siviglia* (Rossini Young Artists) and *Die Zauberflöte* (Lyric Opera Studio Weimar). As a song recitalist, Juliane has been heard at Wigmore Hall, the Barbican, the Purcell Room and on West End stages. She is a current bursary recipient from the Opera Awards Foundation.

Anna Lewis – Set Designer

Anna is an award-winning set and costume designer. She was a Jerwood Young Designer 2016/17 and a recipient of the MGC Futures bursary.

Recent design work includes *Outlying Islands* (King's Head Theatre); *EAST* (King's Head Theatre, currently an Offie finalist for Best Ensemble); *Dangerous Giant Animals* (Underbelly, Winner of the SIT-Up Award); *Life According to Saki* (C Venues, Winner of the Carol Tambor Best of Edinburgh Award which transferred Off Broadway); *A New Coat for Christmas* (Oxford Playhouse, Reading Rep); *After October* (Finborough Theatre, Offie nominated for Best Costume Design). Anna works regularly in the Prop and Costume Departments of the National Theatre and spent much of 2018 working on *The Inheritance* both at the Young Vic and for its West End transfer. She is currently working in the Costume Department of the English National Ballet on *Cinderella* which will be performed at the Royal Albert Hall.

www.annalewistheatredesign.com

David Doyle – Lighting Designer

David is a multi-award winning lighting designer working across the UK and Ireland.

Previous work at the King's Head Theatre includes *Outlying Islands* and *East* (both productions for Atticist) for which he was nominated for an Offie for Best Lighting Design.

Recent work includes: *Richard Carpenter is Close to You* (UK and Australia Tour); *Dangerous Giant Animals* (Winner of the SIT-Up Award); *The Cat's Mother* (Winner of the Fishamble New Writing Award); *Confirmation* (Nominated for the Outburst Award); *Life According to Saki* (Winner of the Carol Tambor Best of Edinburgh Award); *My Name is Saoirse* (Winner of the Best Theatre Award at Adelaide Fringe, the First Fortnight Award, and an Argus Angel); *Substance*, for which he won the NSDF Commendation for Lighting Design. He has also been nominated for several other awards including the Little Gem Award and the Judge's Choice Award at the Dublin Fringe, and the Edinburgh Award at the Edinburgh Fringe. David also works as a theatre producer.

David Eaton – Sound Designer

David studied at the Royal College of Music under Yonty Solomon and Edwin Roxburgh. He has been the Musical Director of Charles Court Opera for over ten years and has worked with them on productions of most of the Gilbert and Sullivan Operettas as well as works by Puccini, Mozart, Ligeti, Peter Maxwell Davies and Rodgers. He has also worked as a lyricist, writer and arranger on the Charles Court Opera Pantomime for the last nine years.

As an accompanist, he has played at concert venues across the country including St. John's Smith Square, the Purcell Room and the Wigmore Hall as well as performing several times live on Radio 3 and BBC Television. He is also a Musical Director for Associated Studios, London and Grims Dyke Opera. Apart from his work on the CCO pantommines, David has also had translations performed at the Grimeborn Festival.

Jennifer Fletcher – Movement Director

Jennifer trained in Dance Theatre at LABAN and has since worked as a Choreographer, Director and Theatre Maker in Opera, Theatre and Film.

Creative credits include *Much Ado About Nothing* & *The Tempest* (Grosvenor Park Open Air Theatre); *As Long as the Heart Beats* (National Theatre Wales); *Semele* (Mid Wales Opera/RWCMD); *Rapunzel* (Cambridge Junction); *People of the Eye* (Deaf & hearing Ensemble); *Dido and Aeneas* (Bath International Festival/RCM);

Wind In The Willows (The Lord Chamberlain's Men). Jennifer co-founded, and continues to make dance and physical theatre work that has been presented in Europe and USA with The Mostly Everything People and NOVA. Both work with multiple disciplines and methods of combining text, movement, live music and language. She is currently developing an original musical with Composer Harry Blake and BRIT School supported by the Andrew Lloyd Webber Bridge Fund, to be premiered in London June 2019. She will also be Associate Director for Don Giovanni at Longborough Festival Opera in 2019.

Alexandria Anfield – Assistant Director

Alexandria is currently a Trainee Resident Director at the King's Head Theatre. Previous credits as Director include *A Working Title* (The Union, Salford Arms, Edinburgh Fringe Festival); *Ruckus in the Garden* (Lowry Theatre); *Man of Mode* (Upstairs at the Gatehouse); *Shark* (Blue Elephant Theatre). As Producer: *A Working Title* (The Union, Salford Arms, Edinburgh Fringe Festival); *Twelfth Night* (Blue Elephant Theatre); *Gone* (Theatre503); Series of New Writing Nights (Blue Elephant Theatre, CentrE17). As Assistant Producer: *Buttons: A Cinderella Story* (King's Head Theatre). Alexandria is also also Artistic Director of Original Impact Theatre Company, an ensemble company that creates new writing.

Louisa Davis – Producer

Louisa Davis is the Senior Producer at the King's Head Theatre. Credits include three West End transfers to Trafalgar Studios including Kevin Elyot's *Coming Clean*, Tommy Murphy's *Strangers in Between* and the Olivier-Award nominated *La bohème*; *Trainspotting*, which enjoyed significant critical acclaim and has gone on to multiple successful seasons at King's Head Theatre, Edinburgh Fringe Festival, at the 777 Theater Off-Broadway in New York as well as UK and international tours; Joe DiPietro's *F*cking Men* at King's Head Theatre, the Vaults Theatre and Edinburgh Festival; *2 Become 1* at King's Head Theatre and Edinburgh Festival; *Hamilton (Lewis)* at the Edinburgh Festival and King's Head Theatre and *(sorry)* at the Edinburgh Festival.

Other credits at King's Head Theatre include Richard Cameron's *The Flannelettes*; *Shock Treatment*, the equal sequel to *Rocky Horror*; the *Cosi* season featuring *Così fan tutte* and Louis Nowra's *Cosi*; the first UK revival of Colin Spencer's *Spitting Image*; *Madam Butterfly*; *The Magic Flute*; *La Traviata*; and the Off West End Award-winning *Tosca*.

Octavia Peneş – Stage Manager

Octavia Peneş is a young Romanian stage manager who graduated National Music University from Bucharest, with a Bachelor degree in Performing Arts. She started her professional life as a violin player and after two years, she applied for an opera stage manager job and got hooked on this beautiful theatrical career. Octavia has extensive experience in stage managing, gained during an eight year contract with the National Opera House in Bucharest. A professional stage manager with excellent communication and team working skills and a friendly attitude, she currently lives in London and enjoys a range of work in the UK and abroad.

Alexander Hick – Assistant Producer

Alexander is a Trainee Resident Director at the King's Head Theatre. He has previously produced *An Abundance of Tims* (Bread and Roses Theatre, Tristan Bates Theatre, King's Head Theatre, Greenside Venues).

His directing credits include *Never Swim Alone* (Etcetera Theatre); *An Abundance of Tims* (Bread and Roses Theatre, Tristan Bates Theatre, King's Head Theatre, Greenside Venues); *Colin Came Instead* (Katzspace); *Company* (Caryl Churchill Theatre, Finalists Festival). He is a founding member of Shepard Tone and Artistic Director of Forge Collective.

King's Head Theatre

The King's Head Theatre was established in 1970. Passionate about championing ethically produced fringe theatre, we are known for our challenging work and support of young artists.

Last year 88,029 audience members saw a show of ours: 37,586 at our 110-seater home on Upper Street and 50,443 elsewhere. At our home in Islington we had 686 performances last year of 113 different shows. We are committed to fighting prejudice through the work we stage, the artists and staff we work with and by producing work for minority audience groups. We believe in fair pay for all on the fringe and create accessible routes for early career artists to stage their work; work we are passionate about.

In 2017, we announced the theatre is on the move. Subject to a fundraising campaign, the King's Head Theatre will move into a custom-built space in the heart of Islington Square, directly behind its current home securing the future of the venue for generations to come.

A Letter from the Artistic Director

Hello! Welcome to the King's Head Theatre

I am delighted that our first opera of 2019 is Georges Bizet's *Carmen*. With some of the world's most beloved music, this highly original new production of *Carmen* depicts this classic in a way never seen before. Carmen has traditionally been portrayed as a femme fatale, but in this new version, we see her as what she is: a young woman who makes the mistake of falling for two different people. The King's Head Theatre continues to radically change the face of opera and support talented emerging artists with a young female creative team led by former Trainee Resident Director Mary Franklin. Our *Carmen* is vivid, compelling and devastatingly powerful, examining toxic relationships in a society on the brink of collapse.

The King's Head Theatre has always been a home for ambitious programming and exciting emerging artists. Last year 88,029 audience members saw a show of ours: 37,586 at our 110-seater home on Upper Street and 50,443 on tour. At our home in Islington we had 686 performances last year of 113 different shows.

But we couldn't do any of this without your support. If you're already a supporter of the theatre thank you so much. If not would you consider signing up? You can become a Friend for just £25 a year. Every Friend and Supporter, as well as all the wonderful audience members who donate money in our bucket, is vital to ensuring we remain accessible for generations to come.

Thank you, enjoy your stay and we hope to see you again soon.

Adam

Adam Spreadbury-Maher
Artistic Director

Support the King's Head Theatre

'In uncertain times, it's great to see one of the stalwarts of London's fringe going onwards and upwards'

Mark Gatiss

The **King's Head Theatre** is an ambitious, thriving producing house located in the heart of Islington. From the emerging companies and creatives, to the thousands of audience members we welcomed through our doors last year, people are at the heart of everything we do.

Famous for an unapologetically broad programme of work and an unwavering commitment to ethical employment on the fringe, the King's Head Theatre occupies a unique place in the capital's theatre ecology.

Each year, the King's Head Theatre needs to raise £100,000 to keep producing and presenting ambitious work that supports, develops and values our artists, staff, audiences and alumni. We hope you will join us on that journey by becoming one of our **Supporters**.

There are three ways to become a Supporter:

Online	www.kingsheadtheatre.com/supporters
By Telephone	0207 7226 8561
In Person	at the box office

For further information or to discuss bespoke packages to suit you, please contact Alan on **friends@kingsheadtheatre.com**

KEY TO THE STAGE DOOR from £150 per year

Priority Booking Period
Exchange and reserve tickets at no extra cost
'KHT Insights email with production news and announcements ahead of the press
Invitations to Supporters Nights including private pre-show discussions
Acknowledgement in our published play texts and programmes
How this gift might help: £275 pays an actor's wages for one week

KEY TO THE DRESSING ROOM from £500 per year

All membership benefits offered with Key to the Stage Door plus:
Invitation to annual 'Behind the Scenes Breakfast' to hear the Artistic Director
share upcoming plans for the King's Head Theatre
Personal booking via the office
How this gift might help: £500 pays for all the costumes for one of our operas

KEY TO THE KING'S HEAD THEATRE from £1,000 per year

All membership benefits offered with Key to the Dressing Room plus:
Invitation once a year to breakfast with the Executive Director
Opportunity to book house seats to sold out shows
How this gift might help: £1,375 supports the Director for one production

ARTISTIC DIRECTOR'S CIRCLE from £2,500 per year

All membership benefits offered with Key to the King's Head Theatre plus:
Playtext signed by the company for each production attended
Invitation to lunch with the Artistic Director once a year
Opportunity to be given a backstage tour of the theatre for you and up to
5 guests finishing with drinks on the King's Head Theatre's stage
How this gift might help: £2,500 pays for the set design for one of our plays

AMBASSADOR from £5,000 per year

**An exclusive chance to be a truly integral part
of the life of the King's Head Theatre
All of the benefits of Artistic Director's Circle plus:**
Invitations to our Press Nights and post-show parties and the chance
to create additional bespoke benefits suited to your interests
How this gift might help: £5,775 pays for actors throughout the rehearsal period

The King's Head Theatre is a registered charity | Charity No: 1161483

King's Head Theatre Staff

King's Head Theatre Timeline

The King's Head Theatre is 48 years old, here are just a few of the highlights of our journey so far...

1970 Dan Crawford founds the first pub theatre in London since Shakespeare's day and the King's Head Theatre is born.

1983 A revival of *Mr Cinders*, starring Joanna Lumley, opens at the King's Head Theatre before transferring to the West End. It goes on to run for 527 performances.

1986 Maureen Lipman stars in the Olivier Award nominated *Wonderful Town* at the King's Head Theatre.

1988 Premier of Tom Stoppard's *Artist Descending a Staircase* opens at the King's Head Theatre before transferring to Broadway.

1991 Steven Berkoff directs and stars in the UK premiere of *Kvetch* at the King's Head Theatre.

1992 Trainee Resident Directors Scheme wins Royal Anniversary Trust Award.

2010 Opera Up Close, founded by Adam Spreadbury-Maher and Robin Norton-Hale become resident company for 4 years.

2011 *La bohème* wins the Olivier Award for Best New Opera Performance.

2015 King's Head Theatre forms a new charity to secure the future of the theatre. *Trainspotting* is first performed at the King's Head Theatre – in August 2017 it hit it's 900th performance.

2016 43,857 audience members see a show at our London home - our highest footfall ever.

2017 King's Head Theatre announces the transfer of *La bohème* & *Strangers in Between* to Trafalgar Studios 2 in London's West End. *La bohème* goes on to be nominated for Best New Opera Production at the Olivier Awards.

2019 King's Head Theatre's production of Kevin Elyot's *Coming Clean* transfers to Trafalgar Studios 2 in London's West End.

2020 King's Head Theatre moves to its new permanent home in Islington Square, securing the future of the venue for generations to come.

Bizet's

CARMEN

OBERON BOOKS
LONDON

WWW.OBERONBOOKS.COM

First published in February 2019 by Oberon Books Ltd
521 Caledonian Road, London N7 9RH
Tel: +44 (0) 20 7607 3637 / Fax: +44 (0) 20 7607 3629
e-mail: info@oberonbooks.com
www.oberonbooks.com

PB ISBN: 9781786827289
E ISBN: 9781786827319

Cover image by Shutterstock

Printed and bound by 4EDGE Limited, Hockley, Essex, UK.
eBook conversion by Lapiz Digital Services, India.

10 9 8 7 6 5 4 3 2 1

ACT I

We are in the outdoor smoking area of an NHS hospital. JOSE, a nurse, cleans, perhaps mopping up something bloody.

JOSE.
This is not what I signed up for, how did I end up here?
Ev'ryone else just passes through
Ev'ryone else just passes through
Just passing through
Ev'ryone else just passes through

Life and death, nothing else is certain, I'm just wasting time.
Losing out, but I don't deserve this, it's a bloody crime.

Just a nurse and not a doctor, not exactly my dream.
Ev'ryone else is better off
Ev'ryone else is better off
All better off
Ev'ryone else is better off
They're better off
They're better off!

JOSE's phone rings. He looks at the screen.

And another call from the missus,
I wonder what's wrong this time.

JOSE answers the call.

Hello? What's up?
Are you still there, with my Mother?

The audience does not hear what MICAELA says on the other end of the call.

[MICAELA.]

JOSE.
No, I can't, I'm at work still.

[MICAELA.]

JOSE.
I'm off soon.
Micaela stay 'til I get home.

[MICAELA.]

JOSE.
Love you too. I will. I really have to go.

JOSE hangs up.

JOSE.
A sick mother to take care of, just another patient.
Ev'ryone gets what they deserve
Ev'ryone gets what they deserve
What they deserve
What they deserve!

JOSE's phone rings again.

JOSE *(Spoken.)*
Hello? … Yes, Doctor. … Actually, I'm about to go on break…
No, that's… It's fine. Yes, I'll order an X-ray. And a– Yes. Ok.

He hangs up.

His phone rings again, but this time he ignores it.

JOSE.
If the call's a moment later, shift change saves me from this
heap.
Always a last minute crisis,
"beep boop boop beep beep boop boop beep"
Doctor wants another X-ray,
she thinks she needs one more look.
Do you think she cares what I say?

4

Checking his watch...

three, two, one... I'm off the hook.

JOSE.
Fin'lly, break.
No more calls to take.
The only moment in the day when I'm alone.
I need a fag.

> *As JOSE takes out a cigarette and begins to smoke, patients can be heard, also having a cigarette.*

PATIENTS.
It's my first one of the day
and the lighter sparks
and I can't quit
but I don't mind after that first drag

Stub it out and then when it's gone
(stub it out and when it's gone)
just grey ash
can't nick another one
I'll just have to find some other vice

All of the bullshit said by doctors is gone
up in smoke

and any hope of a cure not now so strong
up in smoke

All of the shit doctors say
up in smoke
and any hope of a cure
up in smoke
goes up in smoke, yes, up in smoke

Just one more then I'm done for now
(Just one more, I'm done for now)
Just one more!

5

Ah, just one more then I'm done and I see all the shit from
the day disappear
let it go
up in smoke

*CARMEN, a cleaner in the hospital, enters. JOSE is aware of her
from the moment he sees her. She tries to hide something she's been
carrying. She sees JOSE watching her.*

CARMEN.
[Teasing.] Jose, you're looking sad.
In some trouble at home?
You see, this is why
Why I won't get stuck.

JOSE *(Spoken.)*
What about–?

CARMEN.
Alex and me?
We broke up.

I stayed out 'til the sun came up
Took the drunk tube back to his dark flat
My eyes smeared with last night's make-up
But at half ten he'd wanted me back

Had a piss up with my school friends
Nothing wrong with a little fun
He made it clear this was the end
Saw his bad side, I knew we were done

Ah, love! x4

We were stuck on the box set treadmill
But there's so much more that we could do
Just stayed at home and it was killing me
If you want that, I'm not for you

Just stayed at home and it was killing me, yes, it killed me
So if you want that, if you want that, I'm not for you.

My friends say I can't make 'em stay
But I say boys should stop playing men
Your life shouldn't be an ashtray
Don't stub the fag out before the end

I can't play house, I can't pretend
I live my life like today's my last
If it means that I lose a boyfriend
Then he always belonged in the past

Ah, love! x4

We were stuck on the box set treadmill
But there's so much more that we could do
Just stayed at home and it was killing me
If you want that, I'm not for you.

Just stayed at home and it was killing me, yes, it killed me
So if you want that, if you want that, I'm not for you.

Just stayed at home and it was killing me, yes, it killed me
So if you want that, if you want that, I'm not for you.

An ALARM goes off from within the hospital.

JOSE.
What the hell is that noise?

An extremely calm and authoritarian VOICE speaks over the tannoy.
Loosely rhythmic.

VOICE 1.
Red alert. Red alert. This is not a drill.
All free staff, all free staff, please be on alert.
Patients please remain calm.
There is no need for panic.
Patients please remain calm.
There is no need for pa–

Another VOICE cuts over, also on the tannoy. Also speaking.

VOICE 2.
Code Blue.
On call doctor report to O.R. two immediat'ly.

The two tannoy VOICES overlap.

VOICE 1.
If you have info, Staff, Please call the switchboard now.

VOICE 2.
Staff, this is not a drill. Code Blue, Attention staff.
Attention staff. Attention staff. Attention!

VOICE 1 + 2.
Attention staff. Attention staff. Attention staff. Attention staff.
Please call the switchboard now.

A station phone on the wall rings, JOSE picks up the phone.

[PHONE VOICE.]

JOSE.
Tell me what is going on? Do you know who might have done it?

[PHONE VOICE.]

JOSE.
And you got C.C.T.V.?
If I see her anywhere, I'll see if I can restrain her.
Report to security and–

[PHONE VOICE.]

JOSE.
You don't need to tell me twice that this breach is very serious,
and we need to sort it out as quickly as we can.

Yes, I'll call back to report, this is all quite serious.
We'll sort it out, we'll sort it out.
Yes, I'll call back to report.

JOSE hangs up the phone.

CARMEN.
Jose... who was that who just called you?

Come on, tell me who just called you.

Tell me, Jose, what was that all about?
What on earth is code blue tell me, what does that mean?

JOSE.
Someone's stolen some drugs.

CARMEN.
Oh no! How did it happen?

JOSE.
Someone's stolen some drugs.

CARMEN.
Oh no! How did it happen?

JOSE.
And they know who took them!

CARMEN.
Shit that's bad.

JOSE.
Yes, they know who, who is the thief!

VOICE 1 *[over the tannoy.]*
Attention. Red alert, hospital now on lockdown.

JOSE.
Carmen!

CARMEN.
Jose!

CARMEN/JOSE.
Please just listen to me.
I don't know what to do!
Listen to me
Listen to me
Listen to me Carmen/Jose, Carmen/Jose listen to me!

JOSE.
Carmen, what did you do? What the fuck were you thinking?

CARMEN.
Jose, it will be fine, nothing bad is going to happen.

JOSE.
I can't believe you! I can't believe you!

CARMEN.
It will all be fine!
It will all be fine!

JOSE.
No!

CARMEN.
Yes!

CARMEN / JOSE.
Trust me, I know it will be fine.
/ Trust you? Oh no, it won't be fine.

JOSE.
What the fuck did you do?

CARMEN.
I had to make some cash. Yes, yes, yes, yes.

JOSE.
What the fuck did you do?

CARMEN.
I needed cash.

JOSE.
What did you do!

A moment. They size each other up. Eventually, DON JOSE physically restrains CARMEN.

CARMEN.
Tra la la la la la la la la,
So is this how you like it, or are you just teasing?

Tra la la la la la la la la,
You should really get out more, if you catch my meaning.

JOSE *(Spoken.)*
So, why'd you do it? What was the point, Carmen? Don't you care about your job? *(Beat.)*
Fine, don't answer me, you're such a child. I'll just call and tell them I caught you.

CARMEN.
Tra la la la la la la la la,
I can tell you find danger a little displeasing.

CARMEN.
Tra la la la la la la la,
but to act like a rat is just really demeaning.

JOSE.
(Under his breath.) Bitch. *(He makes a phone call.)* Hello? It's about– Yeah, I found Carmen. I have her. By the smoking area on– yeah. Ok. I'll wait.

CARMEN.
Tra la la la la la la

JOSE.
Huh? Yeah, I'm still here. Yeah, I heard. But how long will they– No, I can't I mean... fine. Fine. *(He hangs up.)*

DON JOSE and CARMEN wait in silence. Eventually:

CARMEN.
There's a small place not too far from here, some nights I'm
there until closing.
I go there to dance and to kick off my shoes with a cold beer.
It's my fav'rite place to go out drinking.

Sometimes it can get kind of lonely
and if there's nothing fun to do

I like to bring my boyfriend with me, if you're lucky it might
be you.
Until today, I had someone, good thing I dumped his sorry ass!

Now I can look for someone newer, something more fun than
I had before.
It's time I look'd for someone better,
Someone who will always come through.

I know I've made some crappy judgements,
but not this time; I'm sure it's you.

Can you keep up? I'm quite a handful. Give me a chance you
won't regret,
'cause I need someone just like you to have my back and then
I'll go...

to a small place not too far from here, some nights I'm there
until closing.
I go there to dance and to kick off my shoes with a cold beer.
Yes, It's my fav'rite place to go out drinking.

JOSE.
Shut up!
I really don't care what you have to say!

CARMEN.
I'm just singing a song,
I'm singing to myself
I'm singing to myself
Yes, I'm thinking, if it annoys you, stop listening.

I'm thinking about another man, the kind who could take me away
and give me another life
another life
one better than today.

JOSE.
Carmen!

CARMEN.
He'd be someone who wants all the same things
someone who just understands,
A man who lives life to its fullest appreciates my flaws
He'd be someone who breaks all the rules.

JOSE.
Carmen, I'm confused by what you're saying, but of course
I want to be with you! I could love you, yes, if I loved you...
Carmen, I love you, Carmen tell me you'll be with me.

CARMEN.
Yes...

JOSE.
You will be with me...

CARMEN
Yes, we will drink

JOSE.
you promise?

CARMEN.
and we will dance, we'll be together and go...

JOSE.
You promise me?

CARMEN.
to a small place not too far from here, some nights I'm there
until closing.

I go there to dance and to kick off my shoes with a cold beer.
Tra la la la…

JOSE gets a text message.

DON JOSE.
It's time. They want to speak to you now.

CARMEN.
Please Jose, I'll be deported.
You can just let me go and tell them that I had a knife.
Please trust me, it will work and then we'll be together.
Don't get stuck on the endless treadmill
Yes, there's so much better you could do
Don't play it safe 'cause it will kill you
If you want that, I'm not for you.

Don't play it safe 'cause it will kill you, yes, it will kill you
And if you want that, if you want that, I'm not for you.

JOSE hesitates, then lets CARMEN go.

ACT II

We are in a Karaoke bar. CARMEN, now working as a waitress, cleans.

CARMEN turns on the radio.

FRASQUITA.
It's 10 o'clock at the BBC News desk, I'm Frasquita Jones.
There's a severe weather warning for the North counties this
weekend, with heavy rains and even flooding to be expected.

A 27 year old man, Jose Wilson, has been charged with
stealing thousands of pounds worth of narcotics from the
local hospital where he was employed as a nurse. The man's
accomplice, Carmen Markovi , was also a hospital employee.
Her whereabouts are still unknown. The two were intending,
police believe, to supply the drugs to be sold on the street.
After three weeks in prison, Wilson was released on bail
this morning and is due before a local magistrate's court on
Monday.

A local gang has been implicated in a smuggling operation
with international implications–

CARMEN switches the station. Over the Radio:

CROWDS.
Let's go!
Let's go!
Escamillo!
Let's go!
Let's go!
Escamillo!
Let's go!
Let's go!

RADIO ANNOUNCERS.

BAZ.

Wow! Just listen to those crowds. That clip was recorded earlier today as rising Spanish football star, Escamillo, scored a goal in the final minute of the game against West Ham.

REMY.

Yeah, I don't know about you, Baz, but I just think you can't help but love this guy.

BAZ.

He's really having a fantastic season out there.

REMY.

Now, I don't know if you've heard this, Baz, but Escamillo is, apparently, notoriously difficult for his team manager to control.

BAZ.

Well, he's also one of the many that has some serious superstitions about his game.

REMY.

You know, my favourite's got to be Fabio Borini's classic hand-bite goal celebration.

BAZ.

Coming up after the break, we'll get into the superstitions of Britain's greatest athletes.

REMY.

Oh, go on then, let's hear another clip of those crowds first.

BAZ.

Catchy, isn't it?

CROWDS.

Let's go!

Escamillo!

Let's go!

Let's go!

CARMEN changes the radio station again. She tunes to the Gypsy song, and sings along.

The night has an electric spark
as people search for darkened corners
they linger for a moment longer
and lovers make-out in the dark

The beat demands you dance along
the music moves you to your core,
a verse you're sure you've heard before,
that endless dance, that ceaseless song
that endless dance that ceaseless song

Tra la la …

It seems the music never ends
she's trapp'd within an endless cycle
continuing the upward spiral
she knows she'll never come back down

The dance and song in perfect sync
The dance and song in perfect sync
They pull her in, into the heat
seduce her with heavy beats as they build into a fever pitch!
Tra la la…

ESCAMILLO enters. CARMEN is disinterested and vaguely annoyed to have a customer.

Can I get a cup of coffee, 'cause I'm
Not really fit to drive my Maserati
It's been a long night
Don't worry, I'm alright
Yes, you probably recognise me, please don't make a scene

Looking through the grimy windows
Of this run down Spanish karaoke bar
I almost walked past

I'm glad I turned back
I have never seen a face like yours, ever before

She doesn't buy into it.

You know there's a place around the corner
The service is a little nicer there
They always hold a table for me there
We could go, I could get you in.

She still doesn't go for it.

You mind?

He goes over to the Karaoke machine…

Some Beatles?

CARMEN looks at him with distain.

Or not…
I know!

This is a Karaoke number.

Ah!
Toreador en garde!
Toreador, Toreador
Ay son-gay bee-yen blah blah blah de blah…
I clearly don't speak French
Yes, there are some words here
Toreador!
I've never seen before…

> *CARMEN is trying very hard not to be charmed by ESCAMILLO.*
> *He's a bit embarrassed. He switches songs. It's a croon-y love song*
> *version of "I've Never been in Love Before" from Guys and Dolls.*

I have never been in love before
Now all at once it's you
It's you forevermore

I thought my heart was safe
I thought I knew the score
We don't need no happy endings, we have right now

> *He looks at CARMEN. They have a moment. He forgets about the whole karaoke thing.*

Pour a drink and take a chance with me
I see it in your eyes, you knows there's something here
You're sure you've seen my face
Somewhere you cannot place
I will make sure this moment is not our only one

I sense you're not someone
Who trusts easily
That you might not go for me without assurance
Let me in
You will not regret it
A stranger can be the one

I know
You want me
And I
Want you

Ah!
Tonight's our night
And everything has changed
Tonight's our night
This is our shot
One kiss and there will be no going back
I thought I knew the score
But there is something here
There's something more
Something I can't ignore

CARMEN.
Something here?

ESCAMILLO.
Something here

CARMEN.
Something more?

ESCAMILLO.
Something more

CARMEN.
I'm not sure

ESCAMILLO.
But I'm sure tonight's our night

ESCAMILLO *(Spoken.)*
When does your shift end? Wanna go somewhere?

CARMEN *(Spoken.)*
I can't tonight. I'm waiting for someone.

ESCAMILLO *(Spoken.)*
And if I say I think I'm in love?

CARMEN *(Spoken.)*
I'd say I don't need any more love.

ESCAMILLO *(Spoken.)*
What do you need?

CARMEN *(Spoken.)*
I'll call you when I figure it out.

> *ESCAMILLO and CARMEN exchange numbers. ESCAMILLO exits.*
> *CARMEN returns to cleaning.*

> *CARMEN receives a phone call from her friend, MERCEDES.*

[MERCEDES.]

CARMEN.
I'm at the bar,
what's up with you?

[MERCEDES.]

CARMEN.
Ah, no, I can't,
no, I can't!
I'll come out with you all later.
But tonight I can't, I've got plans
so, I can't go,
no, I can't go! Next time!

[MERCEDES.]

CARMEN.
If you must know, I've got a date! I need to see Jose tonight.

[MERCEDES.]

CARMEN.
I wouldn't call it love… Gotta run!

> *CARMEN hangs up the phone. She can hear JOSE approaching, singing.*

> *JOSE absentmindedly sings a tune as he approaches.*

JOSE.
Break it down, turn around, not just for one night
on the prowl on the town spoiling for a fight
I know that you want me and that I want you too
soon we'll be in love
take things nice and slow
we don't need to rush
love's always a slow burn when you know it's right
find someone who's true, not just for one night!

> *JOSE enters.*

CARMEN *(Spoken.)*
Jose!

JOSE *(Spoken.)*
Carmen, you look… really… beautiful. Why didn't you come–

CARMEN *(Spoken.)*
Don't be an idiot, they'd arrest me. *(Beat.)* It's been a while.

JOSE *(Spoken.)*
Yeah. I came straight here.

CARMEN *(Spoken.)*
What's with the anklet?

JOSE *(Spoken.)*
… Bail conditions. Can't stay out too late. *(Beat.)* I have to
head back soon, Carmen, I –

CARMEN.
Don't be so stress'd, sit down, relax,
and I will dance for you
Have a drink if you'd like,
Or maybe more than just one.

You deserve it, my Jose.
so enjoy it!

La la la la la …

JOSE.
I don't have time, Carmen, I need to make my curfew.

CARMEN.
and you want me to stop?

JOSE.
Just a sec, hang on…
Yes, that is my tag beeping, I need to get back,
oh, please can you just stop.

CARMEN.
Bravo, bravo. That's even better, you know it's hard to keep
the beat without any band, at least now we've got music and it
sounds pretty good.

La la la la la...

JOSE.
You do not understand, Carmen.
I need to get back, or I could go to prison 'cause of you once
again.

CARMEN.
'cause of me?
'cause of me?

Ah, how could I be so stupid?
Ah, how could I be so stupid?
I tried my best for you, you think it's all my fault. I don't
know what you want, I thought you cared for me...
And you're here, so I danced, I thought that's what you'd
want, and now I am the ass.
"beep beep beep beep," he's got a curfew now...
"beep beep beep beep," you'd better hurry back!
Out on bail,
With some bling...
Go!
You need to go check in?
Is that all?
You don't want what is here, so go!
You can leave like they all do.

JOSE.
It's mean of you, Carmen
to think I'd act like that.
If I could stay I would,
and you should know it's true
that I don't want to leave

you know that I would always be with you
there's no one else on earth I'd
rather spend my night with.

CARMEN.
"beep beep beep beep" "I really need to go"
"beep beep beep beep"
"oh no, I'm running late!
Oh my God!
It's my curfew!
I need to check in!
What if I get sent back!"
Well then, just go!
Get lost!
You don't love me at all.

JOSE.
Carmen, how could you think I don't love you?

CARMEN.
You don't!

JOSE.
Oh God! What have I said?

CARMEN.
It's what you did instead.

JOSE.
Listen to me now.

CARMEN.
There is nothing to say.

JOSE.
Listen to me now.

CARMEN.
No, no no no!

JOSE.
Yes! You'll hear me out.
You must listen now! Yes, you will hear.

Ah, long before that day, that hour
when you first handed me that flower…
So many things I wanted to say,
But after work you'd never stay
when I knew you felt the same
I was happy to take the blame,
but now you seem somehow unsure,
again, you've made me so insecure.
I want to hate you or forget you
I know if I don't, I'll regret you,
but all the things you've made me feel,
I know what we have could be something real.
Yes, I know that you aren't good for me
and it was all lies, I can see
Despite all, the things you said,
one thought still runs, runs through my head:
Oh, my dearest Carmen, you owe me.
Please, don't reject me again, Carmen.
I know I couldn't take it if you did,
we are the only choice we have now
Ah, yes, Carmen,
My life is nothing without you!
Carmen, I love you.

CARMEN.
No, this is not true love.

JOSE.
What did you say?

CARMEN.
No, this is not true love.
No, you don't understand that love, that love should set you free.

JOSE.
Carmen…

CARMEN.
Yes, love isn't something you can cage.

JOSE.
Carmen!

CARMEN.
It can't belong to you and me,
If you're in love you'll let it go,
you have to trust in time that it will find you
yes, trust in love will set you free.

Love isn't something you can cage

JOSE.
My curfew!

CARMEN.
it can't belong to you and me.
Yes, trust in love, and you'll be free.

Why do you seem so afraid
Let yourself go, stop trying to be in control
Life's not about all the rules,
We could just leave, there's nothing to keep us here.

Open your eyes and look around,
all of the world can be yours
Let's go away and leave all of this behind…
Then at last we can be together.

We will be free, we will be free.

JOSE.
Oh God…

CARMEN.
Love isn't something you can cage

JOSE.
Carmen...

CARMEN.
it can't belong to you and me

JOSE.
Be quiet!

CARMEN.
If you're in love you'll let it go
you'll trust in time and you'll be free

JOSE.
Ah, Carmen, just stop, just stop.
Carmen, my God.

CARMEN.
If you're in love you'll let it go, you have to trust in time that
it will find you
Yes, trust in love and then you will be free.

JOSE.
No, Carmen, no.

CARMEN.
Let yourself go.

JOSE.
I can't, Carmen.

CARMEN.
You will be free.

JOSE.
No, I can't.

CARMEN.
Ah yes, then we can be together.

JOSE.
Oh, my God, Carmen.

CARMEN.
Love isn't something you can cage
Just trust in love and you'll be free

JOSE.
No, why can't you see?

CARMEN.
Yes, trust in love and you'll be free.

JOSE.
No! I can't do what you want.
If we ran away, and they found where we were...
I'd go to prison!
I can't go back!

CARMEN.
So then, go!

JOSE.
Carmen can't you hear me?

CARMEN.
No! I don't even care!

JOSE.
Please, listen!

CARMEN.
Go! I hate you!

JOSE.
Carmen!

CARMEN.
Goodbye, yes, just go, run back home!

JOSE.
Carmen, you'll regret this… I'll never come back.

CARMEN.
Get out!

JOSE.
Carmen, fuck you! Goodbye, we are done.

CARMEN.
Get out!

> *JOSE is about to leave, but the tag on his ankle beeps again / flashes red. He has missed his curfew deadline. He is defeated. A moment of silence.*

CARMEN.
Jose, what now? You missed curfew…

JOSE.
Now there's no choice!

> *JOSE takes a knife and cuts off the tag and throws it away.*

CARMEN.
Ah, you always have a choice.
That's your problem,
Just stop listening
And you'll be free.

Now we can be together,
leave this behind and start our life
I promise you will never go back to prison.
Yes, the world is what you want to make it
You will be free
You will be free.

JOSE.
Ah!

CARMEN.
Now we can really be together.

JOSE.
I will be free.

CARMEN.
Leave this behind and start our life.

JOSE.
I will be free.

CARMEN / JOSE.
We'll run away to somewhere new
Where they can't find us anymore
And we will start again.
Yes, we will leave this life behind and start again without their
rules, forget the past and we will never look back.
We will be free,
We will be free!

ACT III

JOSE and CARMEN are at a rest stop outside a petrol station. They are living in a car. Their relationship has grown tense and stale. CARMEN is on her phone, texting.

JOSE tries to get physical with CARMEN. She's not into it.

CARMEN.
Just stop. Just stop. I'm not in the mood.

JOSE.
God, Carmen, what the hell's your problem?

CARMEN.
We need to talk, it is important.

JOSE.
Not now, come on, we'll talk later.

CARMEN.
I'm on my period, Jose. I don't want to do this right now.

JOSE.
Carmen, you never do. But, I'll be quick, I'll only be a few minutes.

CARMEN.
Jose–

JOSE.
I'm fine, okay. Living in this piece of shit wasn't my idea.

There is a tense moment. JOSE seems to be waiting for a response. Eventually, he holds out his hand. CARMEN begrudgingly takes out some cash and hands it to him.

JOSE *(Spoken.)*
What the fuck's wrong with you?

CARMEN *(Spoken.)*
I just… need a cigarette.

She lights one. JOSE gets out of the car, and slams the door as he goes.

Eventually, CARMEN, bored, picks up a newspaper that's on the dashboard.

CARMEN.
Ah, look. I'll check my horoscope…

She reads. She gradually becomes more deflated.

Where is it? Pisces…
"It's time to exit while you can
from a close toxic relationship…"

We've been together for months and nothing is better
He hates this gypsy life
Can't go back to his mum but he will not forget her
Wants some submissive wife

"We'll get a little farmhouse in the hills of Spain,
We'll finally settle down."
All of his fantasizing driving me insane
Feel like I'm going to drown

And when I try to go he threatens suicide
I can't escape from him
I know I'm guilty and that I ruined his life
A fight I cannot win

He twists all of my words, 'til I can't tell what's real
He blames it all on me…
I really need to leave
It's time
To go
He's not enough.

CARMEN pulls out her phone and sends a text (to ESCAMILLO).

Outside the petrol station, JOSE, bored and letting off steam, throws rocks at a can.

ESCAMILLO shows up. CARMEN doesn't notice him. She's preoccupied. JOSE almost hits him in the head with a rock.

ESCAMILLO.
A few feet lower down, you would have got my head.

JOSE.
Oh my God, it's you.

ESCAMILLO.
Me? Yeah, I get that a lot.

I'm guessing you watch football? Always nice to meet a fan–

JOSE.
Escamillo!

ESCAMILLO.
That's right.

JOSE.
Yes, I am a big fan!
What are you doing here? I mean we're not exactly inside the M25...

ESCAMILLO.
Yeah, tell me about it...
But I came looking for a girl who wants to meet me. She messaged me to come a couple hours ago, and I just couldn't wait any longer to see her.

JOSE.
Yeah, I know what you mean. Where'd you meet?

ESCAMILLO.
Where'd we meet? When she was working at a bar...

JOSE.
So, what's her name?

ESCAMILLO.
Carmen.

JOSE.
Carmen?

ESCAMILLO.
Carmen, yeah, that's it.

She was with another guy, someone I've never met.
It sounds like they were serious but he's bad for her.

JOSE.
[aside] Carmen!

ESCAMILLO.
She texted me and said that they broke up,
and she asked me to meet her so I came out here.

JOSE.
And you're in love with her?

ESCAMILLO.
I like her.

JOSE.
And she 'likes' you as well?

ESCAMILLO.
I think she likes me, yes. I've never felt this, I think we could
have fun.

JOSE.
But what about the other guy? Aren't you scared of him?
You've shown up here and tried to take her…

ESCAMILLO.
No, she's not mine. It's up to her.

JOSE.
And if this other guy, he won't let you have her?

ESCAMILLO.
He won't let me have her?

JOSE.
You understand?

ESCAMILLO.
That's not really a thing…
This other guy, I think it might be you, yes? I'm sorry if I've made things all weird…

JOSE.
Yes, I'm that guy.

ESCAMILLO.
What a coincidence, what a coincidence…
I'm surprised you're still here.

> *At some point, ESCAMILLO has also started to throw rocks at the can. It has become a competition, and more and more aggressive.*

JOSE.
Oh God, I'm going to kill her, how could she do this?
She lied!
She lied to me for him, she wants him instead of me.

ESCAMILLO.
I thought she broke up with him, so why would he do this?
He really is a dick, she can't want him instead of me.

JOSE / ESCAMILLO.
Let's get this over with, if you want to fight.
Let's get this over with, if you want to fight.
Come on, let's do this, stop fucking around.
Let's do it, I'm not fucking around,
Come on, come on, I'm not fucking around!

The competition reaches its most aggressive point. Just as JOSE is about to attack ESCAMILLO, CARMEN sees and gets out of the car.

CARMEN.
Jose! Please stop! Jose!

ESCAMILLO.
Ah! Carmen, I'm glad I found you.
It's been a while, Carmen, I couldn't wait to see you.
But it looks like I have walked into something private
I wouldn't want to cause any kind of awkwardness…
I just wanted to see if you'd come to my match.

CARMEN.
I'd love to come, I will be there!
But, for now you should go.
Just go, I'll message you later.

ESCAMILLO.
There's one more thing, and then I will give you some space.
I just wanted to say, I'm really glad we met
Since that night I have thought about you constantly.

Give me a call when you can.
Give me a call when you can.

Jose, see you around.

I should go. Yes, I should go!
I'm sure that I will see you soon, so I will say goodbye.

    ESCAMILLO exits.

JOSE.
How could you, Carmen, I should kill you for this!

CARMEN.
Jose, please calm down now, he's gone, it's just us.

Your phone is ringing.

JOSE answers the phone.

JOSE.
Shut up!
Yes, hello? Who is this? Micaela!

MICAELA is on the other end of the phone.

[MICAELA.]

JOSE.
What has happened? Is my mother much worse?

[MICAELA.]

CARMEN.
I think it would be best for both of us if you went back to her.

JOSE.
So you want me to leave you?

CARMEN.
Yes, I think you should go.

JOSE.
'Caela, I'll call you back later.

JOSE hangs up on MICAELA.

I should go? Is that what you want? Yes, I think I understand.
No! I won't go!
Carmen, my mother is dying
All I have is you, there's no-one else.
I need you to help me through this
Yes, without you I won't survive.
Carmen, stop being so selfish,
yes, I need you to be here for me!

JOSE grabs CARMEN. She struggles to get away.

CARMEN.
Let me go!

JOSE.
No, I can't let you go!

CARMEN.
Jose, I'm scared now!

JOSE.
Ah, you are mine, I love you still
and I won't ever let you be with him.
You're the only one I have left.
I know you still love me too.
Carmen, we must be together.
And we don't have any other choice!

JOSE hits CARMEN. It is impulsive and violent.

CARMEN.
Hit me again, why not, I know it's what you want.
Our love, Jose, it never was real.
And you need to know that I kust can't bewith you after this.

JOSE.
Oh God! What have I done!

CARMEN.
You need to go.

JOSE.
Ah yes, I will go!
I'll be back. I'll fix this, it can't be the end.

JOSE leaves. CARMEN is deflated. After a moment, her phone rings.
It's ESCAMILLO. She doesn't pick up, but lets his ringtone play.

ACT IV

We are outside a football stadium. Maybe a large t.v. screen somewhere. We hear a "Match of the Day" style commentary with commentators PAUL, TOM and LUCE.

PAUL. ... When you look back over the last 12 to 14 months of their recruitment, they've spent £350 million pounds on a lot of players, but only £34 million pounds on strikers. And when we're talking about how you qualify for champions league, strikers are the ones who get you into the league. I mean, look at the other team. When you take a player like Escamillo, nobody around him has come anywhere near the types of figures we've seen from Escamillo this season.

TOM. Yeah, Arsenal got really lucky there. Might have something to do with his new girlfriend, this elusive woman he's been seen out with at London's most exclusive clubs or the past few months.

LUCE. Apparently she was a waitress before they met...

TOM. I mean, I wouldn't turn down a night with Escamillo. Going back to this replay, at the start of last week's game they were just fantastic. Dynamic, really playing off each other...

LUCE. And we like to see this kind of effort from a team. Let's take a look at the team's line ahead of this vital clash. Here's a replay from earlier this month. That first goal attempt, a really square pass there from Dancairo in front of the goal. This presented such an easy chance for Escamillo...

PAUL. Yeah, and then looking at another chance, a really good play there, the centre-forward slips a pass in past the defender, Zuniga, and in for his strike partner.

LUCE. Time after time, we're seeing these boys are just able to cut through the defence. Here's another goal, by Remendado this time. We can see it's a fantastic side-foot finish.

TOM. And on that note, stay tuned, and we'll be right back with Harry Kane to get us underway.

The commentary goes to a commercial break.

KID'S VOICE.
"¡Odio la lluvia! Londres es el peor!"

ANNOUNCER.
Tired of that dreary British drizzle?
Fly to Seville and 7 other Spanish destinations from London Gatwick for just 20 pounds with EasyJet. Visit Easyjet.co.uk and...

Experience the sun. Experience Spain. (Some conditions apply.)

SUNG.
Twenty quid, yes! Twenty quid, yes! Twenty quid, yes! Twenty quid, yes!

FOOTBALL FANS can be heard in the distance.

FOOTBALL FANS *(Off.)*
Here they come! Here they come!

Yes, look, here they come!

Here they come, I'm just so excited! I can't wait until the match starts!
Arsenal is so going to win this! Hurrah, hurrah, hurrah! Hurrah! I need to go get a pint first...
I'll nip out before Escamillo...

Here they come, we're so going to win this!
Escamillo! Escamillo! Escamillo!

Tonight's our night, make it happen Escamillo
Tonight's our night, this is our shot
One kick and there will be no going back
He always knows the score!

Go Escamillo!
Go Escamillo!
Ah, Go!

A private moment, ESCAMILLO prepares to head in for the game.

ESCAMILLO.
If you love me, Carmen
You are everything I need
And there is nothing else, you are my lucky charm
If you love me like I love you.

CARMEN.
I don't know, Escamillo, how I could live without you,
with you I've found my home, and I'm completely free.

CARMEN / ESCAMILLO.
Ah, I love you. Yes, I love you.

ESCAMILLO.
Now, Carmen, I really have to go!

ESCAMILLO exits. CARMEN gets a phone call from MERCEDES.

[MERCEDES.]

CARMEN.
Hey, did you find your seats?

[MERCEDES.]

CARMEN.
Jose?

[MERCEDES.]

CARMEN.
Not in the stands?

[MERCEDES.]

CARMEN.
I am not afraid of an asshole like him.
I'll be fine. I'll just get him to leave.

[MERCEDES.]

CARMEN.
I'll see you soon. Ten minutes.

CARMEN *(Spoken.)*
I have to go.

    CARMEN hangs up. JOSE enters.

CARMEN.
You're here.

JOSE.
I'm here.

CARMEN.
My friends told me that I shouldn't talk to you alone, they
think that it's not safe.
Yes, Mercedes worries that you might hurt me. But I'm not
scared, there's no reason to fear.

JOSE.
No, I would never hurt you.
Believe me, I'm not like that.
Yes, I love you, Carmen, and I have changed.
I am better.
Yes, I knew when I hurt you that I needed to get better.
Now it's time that we move on.

CARMEN.
You think I could be with you now after everything you did?

We were done before you hit me. I can't forgive. I never will.
So, please, could you just go?
We are through, you shouldn't stay.

JOSE.
Carmen, I know you don't mean that.
Yes, I get that you're angry, but my Carmen, we will start
over now, I am so sorry.
Oh, this can't be the end of us, I don't think it's what you
want.

CARMEN.
Yes, I have made my decision, and now you, you need to
listen.
I don't want to see you again. No, No!
Now you need to get away from me.

JOSE.
Carmen, I know you don't mean that.

CARMEN.
What else could I mean?

JOSE.
I got help, I went to counc'ling.

CARMEN.
Listen, that does not mean that we are okay.

JOSE.
I know that I can give you everything you've ever wanted.
Oh, we can still escape this life.
We'll run away just like we planned.

CARMEN.
No, we have already tried.

JOSE.
Oh, my Carmen, I know you'll regret it, oh, this can't be the
end of us, Carmen.

CARMEN.
Oh please, Jose. You need to hear what I have to say, there is nothing left and we are done.

JOSE.
Oh, this can't be the end of us, Carmen, I love you. I don't think it's what you want.

CARMEN.
I'm already gone, it's what I want.

JOSE.
So, you think I should leave?
Yes, you want me to go?

CARMEN.
Yes. I can't see you again.

JOSE.
I lost my job and went to prison for you
And now, now you don't even give a shit.

CARMEN.
I'm sorry, Jose, but it was your choice.

JOSE.
And now, all you want is money and wealth.
Yes, it is all your fault.
I gave up everything.
And now you're leaving me.
You ruined me, you wanted this.
Ah, Carmen, I know that you're not sorry.
Stop crying now! It's all a lie, I see.
You wanted this to happen.
Ah, you'll always be mine Carmen and there is nothing else.

CARMEN.
I didn't make you do those things.
No, it was not my fault, it was your choice!

JOSE grabs CARMEN and they struggle.

FOOTBALL FANS *(Off.)*
Watch him cut straight through their defences! There is
nothing that can stop him!
Oh no, Nine, look out, he's behind you! Man on, man on,
man on,
Man on! Oh no! This is a disaster.
I don't think Lacazette's going to make it!
Oh my God, but there's Escamillo!
Man on! Man on! Man on!
He'll save it!

JOSE.
So, it's him!

CARMEN.
Who do you mean?

JOSE.
You want to be with him and I'm not good enough.

CARMEN.
I must go! I must go!

JOSE.
I can't let you. I cannot let you go,
Carmen, why do you want to leave?

CARMEN.
Let me go, please, Jose, I cannot be with you!

JOSE.
Is it because of him?
Say it. And look at me!

CARMEN.
I love him!
So hit me, since that's what you like, but I swear that I'll never
love you!

FOOTBALL FANS *(Off.)*
Oh my God, look out Escamillo! Did you see that? God, what a head-butt!
See, he's bleeding, oh no! He's injured! Oh no, oh no, oh no
Oh no! It looks like he can't get up now
What will they do without Escamillo?!

JOSE.
It's clear, that's what you really think then.
You will run to him and then you, then you will forget me, you slut!
When you're with him, you'll laugh at me!
I swear to God, you'll never go, Carmen.
You will be with me!

CARMEN.
No, no, Jose.

JOSE.
I cannot let you be with him!

CARMEN.
I hate myself for ever being in love with you!

FOOTBALL FANS *(Off.)*
Escamillo!

JOSE.
For the very last time, Carmen, say that you want me.

CARMEN.
No, no! I will never be yours, Won't you leave me alone. Go!

JOSE.
I can't!
I can't!

FOOTBALL FANS *(Off.)*
Tonight's our night, make it happen Escamillo
Tonight's our night, this is our shot

One kick and there will be no going back
He always knows the score!
Yes, there is something here
There's something here
We've never seen!

JOSE kills CARMEN.

JOSE.
You said you'd be with me! I know that you loved me…
Yes, you promis'd. You are mine and no-one else's…

END.